AWARD PUBLICATIONS – LONDON

# Tinker goes skating

LUCIENNE ERVILLE · MARCEL MARLIER

It was wintertime. Rusty the little dog with the long ears had some news for his friend Tinker the kitten.

'Joseph the gardener says it's going to freeze! He says that in three days the water in the pond will be so hard that we can walk on it!'

Joseph began to take his pots of flowers into the shed for shelter. Then he took the basket that Rusty and Tinker slept in, and put that in the shed as well.

'You'll be more comfortable here than in the garden,' he said to Rusty 'And you'll have your friend, too.'

The two little animals were delighted at the idea of living together in the shed.

Joseph was right. It began to get colder and colder. For the first
two days in the shed, Rusty and Tinker invented all sorts of new
games. In between they ate as much as they could.
At night they dreamed about flying over the ice.

'I think flying might be easier than walking,' said Tinker when
they woke up.
On the third day Rusty had had enough of staying indoors.
He couldn't keep still.
'I want to go to the pond,' he said.
Tinker pretended to be deaf.
At last Rusty ventured out of doors,
but he was soon back, growling:
'That frost! It stings and it bites
and you can't see it!'

Tinker looked out of the shed window to see what was going on
outside. There was no sign of life. Nothing moved.
'Look at the trees, Rusty  Poor things they're quite bare, all stiff
and white with frost. If we go outside perhaps we shall go all
stiff, like the trees!'
So the two friends stayed indoors, feeling restless and unhappy.
Suddenly they heard the noise of the gardener's wheelbarrow,
squeaking up the path. Joseph pushed the door open.
'Come on, you two! The pond is frozen. Out you go!'
All their fears disappeared. When Joseph was there they knew
that nothing terrible would happen to them.

He picked the two friends up very gently by the backs of their necks and dropped them in the middle of a heap of dry leaves in the barrow.

It made a lovely, crackly nest. The leaves kept them warm and they quite stopped shivering.

Two ducks who were watching were full of envy and quacked : 'Some people have all the luck!'

MARLIER M.

Pulled by the kind Joseph, the wheelbarrow jog-trotted across the garden towards the pond.

There was not the tiniest flower left in the borders, not even one leaf left on the apple tree that had been laden with lovely red apples in the autumn. It was cold and bleak.

But suddenly the sun came from behind the clouds and the garden was completely changed. The frosty trees sparkled and every blade of grass on the lawn looked like beautiful shining glass. The two friends were so excited!

The barrow came to a halt at the edge of the pond.

'All change!' shouted Joseph, who was enjoying himself just as much as Rusty and Tinker.

The two little animals looked at the pond. They couldn't believe that it could have changed so much.

'It's all white. It looks as if someone had filled it with milk!' said Tinker.

'I'd like some to drink!'

Two blackbirds and a family of sparrows landed on the frozen pond.

Joseph picked up a large stone and threw it as far as he could into the middle of the pond. It curved into the air and the blackbirds and sparrows flew off. The stone fell on to the ice, bounced once or twice and came to a standstill.

'Good! The ice is thick enough..Off you go!'

Tinker rushed forward, but he had hardly got on to the ice before he slipped, slid, lost his balance and landed on his back. Rusty was more careful. By taking very small steps he was able to reach Tinker, help him on his feet and brush him down. The kitten felt rather dizzy, but after a lick here and a lick there he began to feel more like himself again.

Then, holding carefully on to each other, Rusty and Tinker began
to slide over the smooth ice.
'I say, I like this, don't you?'
'Yes, it's super,' replied Rusty yapping happily.

They were making so much noise that some of the neighbouring dogs—old Rover, Fritzi the dachshund and Lightning the greyhound—looked over the wall to see what was happening.

'Look! Rusty and Tinker are walking on the pond!'

Miss Sarah's cat, Snow-White, pushed her three kittens forward so that they could get a good view of the fun.

'Why don't we go too?' she suggested.

'Yes, yes, do let's!' clamoured the kittens, all mewing at once.

So the seven friends jumped down from the wall one by one.

Tinker and **Rusty** were getting used to the ice now. They were delighted to have some visitors.

Quite soon they were organising games, pushing each other, falling over and all enjoying themselves enormously.

'Why don't we have a dance on the ice?' suggested Lightning.
'Like they do in ice-shows. But we haven't got any music.'
'Music? We'll look after that,' sang the sparrows, who were perched along the branch overhead.
And they gaily started to whistle a waltz tune.

After the waltz it was time for racing. Rover was the judge.
'Now you little ones, stand here ten paces from the edge. I'm
giving the others a handicap. One, two, three, GO!'
Off they went, but it was Tinker who got to the other side of the
pond first! Everybody crowded round to congratulate him;
everybody shouted. What a noise!

The sun was sinking behind a big cloud and suddenly it was very cold. Joseph had finished tidying the garden. He had made a heap of leaves and branches that was as tall as himself. He

carefully struck a match and put a light to it. The flames leapt up. Tinker, Rusty and their friends all gathered round to watch. The bonfire crackled, and gave out a wonderful heat. But gradually all the leaves and branches burned down to embers, and the fire flickered out. It was time to say goodbye. Everybody went home happy and hungry. Exercise is so good for you!